Scan this QR code
to read online!

Mom's Favourite Boy

Shourya is a 7-year-old boy living in the UK with his family. He is a responsible child, always eager to learn new things. He was his mom's favourite, not just because he was her son, but because of his disciplined nature and love for reading.

One autumn morning, Shourya woke up late. He quickly brushed his teeth, finished is potty, took bath and ate his healthy breakfast, wore his school uniform, and rushed outside where his dad was waiting with the electric scooter.

On his way to school, Shourya saw Percy Pig standing by the roadside. Percy Pig was distributing flyers to all the school kids, inviting them to a book show.

Shourya was excited. He took the flyer from Percy Pig and couldn't wait to show it to his mom. He knew she would be thrilled to go to the book show.

After school, Shourya rushed home.
He shared the news with his mom and
little sister. They were all excited
about the book show.

The day of the book show arrived. Shourya and his little sister, hand in hand, walked into the big hall filled with books of all kinds.

Shourya was amazed. He could see books of all genres. There were books about space, dinosaurs, fairy tales, and even recipe books for kids.

He ran his fingers through the different books, trying to decide which ones to choose. His eyes twinkled with joy and excitement.

Finally, he picked a few books about space and dinosaurs, a fairy tale book, and a recipe book for kids. He also picked a LEGO set.

Shourya's parents were pleased with his choices. He had chosen books over a Nintendo switch. They were proud of their son's love for reading and learning.

After the book show, Shourya couldn't wait to start reading his new books. He opened the dinosaur book and started reading it aloud to his little sister. After reading the Shourya learnt that there were more than 700 different species. Dinosaurs were a diverse group that included both herbivorous and carnivorous species. Some of the well-known dinosaur groups include theropods (like Tyrannosaurus rex), sauropods (like Brachiosaurus), ornithopods (like Triceratops), and many others.

His sister listened attentively, her eyes wide with curiosity. Shourya explained everything to her in a simple language, making sure she understood every bit. And in that moment, as they sat together surrounded by the wonders of the universe, it became clear just how much they loved and cared for each other. The bond between Shourya and his sister was as strong as the gravitational pull of the planets, a love that stretched beyond the stars and back.

After reading, it was time to play with the LEGO set. Shourya and his sister started building a castle. They were having a lot of fun.

That night, Shourya went to bed feeling happy and content. He had a day full of fun and learning. He was looking forward to the next day.

The next morning, Shourya woke up early. He picked up his space book and started reading it. He was fascinated by the stars, the planets, the asteroids, the solar system, Meteoroids, galaxies. As Shourya turned the pages, he discovered the secrets of the solar system. Meteoroids raced through space, and galaxies stretched out like shimmering blankets of stardust. Did you know that the solar system isn't just a boring bunch of rocks? No way! It's a swirling disc of dust and gas!

Later that day, he shared his knowledge about space with his friends at school. They were all impressed by his knowledge. Shourya felt proud.

Days turned into weeks, and weeks into months. Shourya kept learning new things from his books.

His parents noticed a positive change in him. He was more confident, more knowledgeable, and more creative. They were proud of their son.

One day, Shourya's mom asked him if he regretted not buying the Nintendo switch. Shourya smiled and said, "No, mom. I am happy with my books and LEGO."

His mom hugged him tightly. She was proud of her son's maturity and wise choices. She knew she had raised a responsible and wise boy.

Shourya continued his journey of learning and exploring. He knew that books were his best friends. They helped him understand the world better.

He also realized that playing with LEGO helped him improve his creativity and problem-solving skills. He was glad he chose books and LEGO over a Nintendo switch.

Shourya's story is a reminder that books are a treasure trove of knowledge. They can take us to places we have never been and teach us things we never knew.

It also reminds us that toys like LEGO can help in developing a child's creativity and problem-solving skills. It's not always about electronic games.

Shourya's mom was right. He was indeed her favourite boy. Not just because he was her son, but because he was a responsible, mature, and wise boy.

As Shourya grew older, his love for books and learning never diminished. He continued to make his parents proud with his wise choices and mature outlook.

And so, Shourya's journey of learning and exploring continued. With books and LEGO by his side, he was ready to face the world with confidence and knowledge.

The End.

Printed in Great Britain
by Amazon

38107942R00039